Lincoln Branch Library
1221 E. 7 Mile
Detroit, MI 48203

FEB 2009

For George, Katriona, Luke, Rachel and Christian – G.S.
Pour Marie-Julia – S.B.

Text copyright © 2008 by Gillian Shields
Illustrations copyright © 2008 by Sebastien Braun

All rights reserved. Except as permitted under the U.S. Copyright Act of 1976, no part of this publication may be reproduced, distributed, or transmitted in any form or by any means, or stored in a database or retrieval system, without the prior written permission of the publisher.

First U.S. Edition: December 2008

First published in Great Britain by Orchard Books, a Hachette Livre UK company, in May 2008.

Little, Brown and Company

Hachette Book Group USA
237 Park Avenue, New York, NY 10017
Visit our Web site at www.lb-kids.com

LB kids is an imprint of Little, Brown and Company Books for Young Readers, a division of Hachette Book Group USA. The logo design and name, LB kids, are trademarks of Hachette Book Group USA.

Library of Congress Control Number: 2007941434

ISBN: 978-0-316-03273-5

Manufactured in Malaysia

10 9 8 7 6 5 4 3 2 1

The Beginner's Guide
to
Bears

Gillian Shields   Sebastien Braun

LITTLE BROWN & COMPANY
LB kids™
NEW YORK BOSTON

You need a bear
and a bear needs you.
Together you'll share
a friendship that's true.

W

hat kind of teddy bear is right for you?

Some are **big** and cuddly,

others are small with fuzzy hair.

One is waiting
just for you,
ready for tender,
loving care.

A bear is a friend
all seasons of the year.
It's always nice
to have your teddy near.

What things can you and a bear do?

Build castles in the sand,
watch the ducks float by,

make a frosty snowbear,
and fly kites up high.

Bears love playing, bears love toys, bears love making lots of NOISE!

What toys do bears like best?

Dress-up clothes,

balls to throw,
and best of all,
fast carts that *GO!*

When you are hurt,

or sick,

or sad,

only your teddy

can make you glad.

W

hat do bears do
when they don't feel well?

They visit the doctor,

then go home to rest

until they're back
to feeling their best.

Bears love all things
good and yummy.
Picnics are best
for a bear's hungry tummy.

What foods do bears love eating most?

Jelly beans and lollipops, honey-glazed treats . . .

bears aren't picky,
but they *do* like their sweets!

W hen it's late
and time for bed,

be sure to cuddle
with your favorite Ted.

W hat do bears do when it's bedtime?

Grab their blankies,
snuggle up tight,

share a story,
then say, "Nighty night."

E veryone loves
a big bear hug,
soft and cozy,
warm and snug.

W
ho needs a bear?

You need a bear!
And a bear needs *you*.

You and a bear
together make **two**!